My
SWEDISH
Greta

MILF Seduction

Hot Cougar Erotica

JACK RYDER

WARNING

This book contains sexually explicit scenes and adult language. It may be considered offensive to some readers. This book is for sale to adults ONLY.

* * * * * * * * * * * * * * * * * * *

Please store your files wisely where they cannot be accessed by underage readers.

Please feel free to send me an email. Just know that these emails are filtered by my publisher. Good news is always welcome.

Jack Ryder - **jack_ryder@awesomeauthors.org**

You might also want to check my blog for Updates and interesting info.
http://jack-ryder.awesomeauthors.org

About the Publisher

4Fun Publishing, a member of **BLVNP Incorporated**, 340 S. Lemon #6200, Walnut CA 91789, info@blvnp.com / legal@blvnp.com

NOTE: Due to the highly emotional reaction of some people to works of erotic fiction, any email sent to the above address that contains foul language or religious references is automatically deleted by our anti-spam software and will not be seen. All other communications are welcome.

DISCLAIMER

Please don't be stupid and kill yourself. This book is a work of FICTION. Do not try any new sexual practice that you find in this book. It is fiction and not to be confused with reality. Neither the author nor the publisher or its associates assume any responsibility for any loss, injury, death or legal consequences resulting from acting on the contents in this book. Every character in this book is over 18 years of age. The author's opinions are not to be construed as the opinions of the publisher. The material in this book is for entertainment purposes ONLY. Enjoy.

MY SWEDISH GRETA

MILF Seduction

Hot Cougar Erotica

By: Jack Ryder

©Jack Ryder 2014
ISBN: 978-1-62761-883-0

Chapter 1

I knew that Greta was the sexiest MILF I would ever meet from a very early age. She married my father when I was ten years old which was a little more than a year after my mother was killed in an automobile accident. Dad met Greta in a grief counseling group.

Greta was only twenty years old when she married my 32 year old father. She was originally from Sweden and had married a young US Army officer just after she turned eighteen. He had just moved Greta to the US before being deployed to Afghanistan. He was killed by a roadside explosive device just weeks after his deployment.

I never did understand why Greta married my dad. He was such a prudish and authoritarian sort of a man and Greta was just the opposite. She was the most free – spirited and uninhibited person that I have ever met. There were many objections by my father concerning her habit of walking around the house in just her transparent underwear or just a transparent robe. These chastisements usually ended with Greta telling my dad that she would be completely naked if she were home in Sweden. This always got a rise out of me. Literally!

Needless to say, I spent my teenage years fantasizing about my sexy Swedish stepmother. Aided by her transparent underwear and transparent robes, I practically had every inch of her gorgeous body memorized by the time I graduated from high school. Although I had never seen her completely nude, I had seen every inch of her through the shear fabrics she chose to wear around the house. I knew exactly what her puffy pink nipples looked like. I knew where the tiny mole was on her left breast. I knew where the small egg – shaped birthmark was on her right inner thigh just inches from her pussy. I knew that she shaved her pussy bare.

I did get to see her naked once. It was the day I left for Army boot camp. I had gotten up early that morning to ensure I had plenty of time to shower and shave before catching my flight for basic training. I decided to enlist in the Army just after I turned 18 to receive the training that could take many years at a college. I was enlisted as a communications specialist.

I was just rinsing the shampoo out of my hair when I heard the bathroom door open and then close again. "I want you to have something to remember," it was Greta's voice from just outside the sliding glass shower door. As I opened the door, she untied the front of her robe and pulled it open to expose her naked body to me.

"I want you to remember me, Trevor." She said it very softly as she held her robe open for me. "I want you to think about me while you're gone." I could see that her nipples were fully erect and there was a slight glistening between her thighs from her arousal. I could also see that she was staring at my 9 inch dick that had quickly swelled to full rigidness as I gawked at her. "I'm happy that I could please you," she whispered as she pulled her robe closed. "Please come back to me safe, Trevor." Her voice trembled as she said it. "I couldn't bear to lose you like...Scott." I had never heard her say his name before.

I frantically jerked myself as soon as she left the room. I could smell the musky scent of her sex lingering in the small bathroom. I could clearly see every inch of her naked body as I stroked. She had me so aroused that I shot my load all over the shower wall in less than two minutes. I was going to clean up my mess, but with my father out of town on business, she would be the only one to see the discharge I left on the wall. It would let her know how deeply I had wanted her.

Greta kissed me at the door when I was about to leave. It was a hungry desperate sort of kiss. It was not a motherly kiss on the cheek. It was a kiss I would remember every day for the next three years. It was a kiss that made me crave more of her and despair that I had to leave her. It was a kiss that made my heart palpitate and made my dick swell to full glory. "You better come back to me, Trevor," she whispered it in my ear.

It was the last time we would be together for the next three years of my enlistment.

The first two years flew by in a blur. By the end of the first, I was highly proficient at my job as a communications specialist. By the end of the second year, I was expert that everyone in the unit would seek for help with any problem that might arise. It was at this same period of time that I discovered a way to link up on a secret satellite to use as a free and secret Skype link up to anywhere I wanted at any time.

It was Greta that I contacted first. I left her an email to let me know when she would be alone. When I received her answer, I was thrilled. It would be the first time in two years that we would communicate face to face. Up to this point, I had stayed in contact with her through a series of post cards and greeting cards.

"You look wonderful," I gasped when she appeared on my laptop screen. She was wearing her peach colored chiffon robe that is my favorite. I could clearly see both of her puffy nipples through the transparent fabric. "I think you should just call me Greta from now on," she chuckled.

"I have missed you so much," I told her. "I do think about you every day...and in every dream," I was quite surprised that I blurted that last part so openly.

Greta moved closer to her screen so her face was close up on my monitor. "I have thought of you every minute of every day, Trevor," she whispered it. "And I remember that special present you left me that last day every time I take a shower." It took several seconds for that memory to come back to me. How I had left my semen all over the shower wall. I could feel a slight little wiggle between my legs as I remembered it.

"Oooh...Thaaaat," I chuckled nervously. Even on her laptop screen she could see my face turning a bright radiating red. "You have nothing to be embarrassed about," she laughed it joyfully. "I was pleased that you wanted to do that after looking at my naked body," she smiled at me playfully. "Would you like to see it again, baby?" Before I could tell her yes, she stood up and untied her robe. This time, she let it fall off to the floor.

"Oh Greta...you are so lovely," I whispered. Her nipples got hard instantly and so did my cock.

"I have remembered you every...day." I gasped. I had to stop myself from saying I remembered her every time I jerked off. She moved her screen down so I had a close up of her pussy. "Do think of me when you...make a mess?" she giggled it softly. "Oh God Yes...every day," I moaned my reply.

"Good," she laughed playfully. "I think of you every time I do this." She pressed two fingers against her pussy lips and shoved them in as far as they would go. "Ooooh Trevor," she moaned in a sultry voice. "This is what I did that day...when I saw your present," her voice trembled as she pulled her hand back and then shoved the fingers back in. "Ooooh Greta," I moaned as I slipped my hand inside my sweat pants to touch my throbbing prick.

"Let me see it Trevor..pleeeeeze let me see it," she sat in her chair and moved the screen so I could see all of her including her fingers ramming in and out of her sex hole. I quickly shoved my sweat pants down to my knees and adjusted my screen so she could see all of me too. "Oh Trevor...look at you, baby," she gasped. "God, I wish I could feel that inside me," she moaned. I was so aroused that the precum was flooding out of my pee hole and lubricating my cock.

"Yes baby...jerk it off for me, baby," her voice was trembling with excitement as she frantically finger fucked herself for me. "Make a mess for me baby...cum for me...cum for me," she panted.

"Oh Yes Greta...God I want you...God I want you," I moaned as I felt the load building up in my balls. "I want to fuck you Greta...I want to fuck you," I bellowed as I began to ejaculate. As three huge ropes of semen shot out of my prick, I saw Greta shudder as she brought herself off too.

"Yes baby...I want to fuck you too," she gasped. I shot off a fourth time as she confessed that.

We were both just sitting there both naked and fully exposed to each other as we panted for air afterward. Greta looked even more beautiful to me in that moment than ever before. "I hope this doesn't change how you feel about me," I mumbled stupidly. The sound of Greta's belly laugh was music to my soul. "Of course it changed how I feel, silly," she chuckled. "Now I am going to crave your big cock in my pussy every minute of every day," she added.

"You better come back to me, Trevor," she whispered as she was putting her robe back on. "I cannot imagine not having you in my life," she bent her face close to the screen. "Can we do this again?" she giggled. Before we logged off, we agreed on one day each week when we could hook up on Skype and play together. It was just before we closed that she told me that she was pretty certain that dad was cheating on her.

Chapter 2

Shortly after I discovered the secret satellite link that I could use for private Skype chats, one of my buddies noticed that I disappeared every Wednesday night for an hour or so. That was the set time I had to meet Greta on-line to masturbate together. I never heard him come into my tent while I was jerking off with her that night. Because he was far enough behind me, Greta did not see him either. "Wow, that was fucking hot," Jimmy gasped after we both got off.

I nearly fell out of my chair as I twirled around to face him. "GET OUT!" I shouted at him. After he left, Greta told me that it made her pussy wet knowing that he had watched us. I got so aroused by her suggestion that I let others watch us, that we jerked off again before we logged off. Greta made me promise that I would let some other people watch us having sex with each other. "As many as you like," she added.

The following Wednesday night, I had twelve other fellas crowded into my tent. They all had their pants down to their knees and were stroking themselves as Greta and I jerked off together. They all paid me $50 each for the experience. Greta got so aroused that night that she wet herself when she climaxed. After they all filed out of my tent, she confided that it was the first time she had ever squirted.

Things went fairly smoothly over the next couple of months. I had ten or twelve of the fellas that would pay me the $50 to watch Greta and I masturbate with each other. I assured them I was going back home just as soon as this enlistment is over.

Just before Christmas, I received a small package from Greta. Inside, there was a pair of black transparent bikini panties sealed inside a ziplock baggie. There was a note taped on the baggie.

"Baby...I snuck into your room last night when your dad was asleep. These are the panties I was wearing when I masturbated in your bed. I hope you can still smell me in them...Enjoy, Baby!"

My dick was rock hard as I took them out of the bag and held them to my face. I could smell the wonderful fragrance of her Honeysuckle perfume mixed with the muskiness of her sex. I pulled my dick out and jerked off while I sucked on the crotch of her panties.

It was so easy to envision her in these panties and imagine her fingers drilling in and out of her juicy wet snatch. I could hear her moaning my name as I stroked myself frantically. When I felt my load racing for escape, I held the panties in front of my cock and sprayed my cum all over the crotch of her sexy panties. I placed them back in the baggie the next day after the mess had time to dry. Otherwise, it would have been a sour mess when she received it. I mailed it back to her.

It was two weeks later that she announced that she had received her special present. I heard all of the fourteen fellas behind me groan in unison as she lifted the panties to her mouth and start to suck on the crusted cum all over the crotch. "Oh yes,....suck my dick," I gasped as I began to jerk my dick for her. "Yes baby, I'm gunna suck you every day when you come home," she purred as she licked the crotch of her panties. I heard a couple of the guys groan as they blew their loads all over the floor.

"I want to fuck you Greta...I want to fuck you so bad," I groaned. I heard a couple of more guys grunt as they shot off. Greta pulled out a dildo and shoved it into her gash. "Yes baby, fuck me, fuck me," she groaned as she drilled the plastic dick in and out of her gash.

"Give me your seed," she moaned in a very husky tone. I could hear the rest of the guys behind me groaning as they shot off. "Here it is...here it is," I bellowed as I blew my load all over the keyboard of my laptop. "Oh geeeeezus, that was nasty," one of the fellas gasped softly.

"I really do want to fuck you, Greta," I told her quietly as the guys filed out of my tent. "We will definitely make that happen...as soon as you come back to me," she answered me.

I made so much extra cash from our shared sex play during that last year, I was able to let all of my service pay go directly into savings. Since I had already saved nearly half of my first two years pay, I had a very nice bank account waiting for me when I returned to the US. I stopped in Germany for a month prior to my rotation back to the States for final discharge. I purchased a brand new Mercedes sports coupe while I was there and had it shipped home.

My new Mercedes was waiting for me in Charleston South Carolina when I arrived at the airport. So was Greta. She told my dad that she wanted to take a vacation with me and help me drive all the way home. Dad had no clue about the nature of our relationship. He was just pleased that he would have a couple of weeks with his secret girlfriend. He seemed pleased that Greta took such an interest in his only son.

"Oh My God, look at you," I gasped as she approached me at the airport terminal. I forgot how absolutely gorgeous my Swedish stepmom is in person. She was wearing a very sexy and very tight white tube dress. Her long athletic legs looked fabulous as she walked toward me in her four inch heels. Her perky 34B tits pressed so firmly into the fabric of her dress that I could see the contour and upturn of each breast. My dick was swelling quickly as she fell into my arms and kissed me very passionately.

Her long white blond hair hung down her back all the way to the crack of her rear end. I let my hands touch the hollow along her back as I slowly moved them down to fondle her ass. "I have missed you so much, baby," she whispered it in my ear. I noticed that there were several men that had stopped to gawk at us as I gently fondled her. "That feels so good," she moaned. I felt her shudder a little bit as I kissed the side of her neck. "Let's go get a room," I suggested softly.

I revealed in all the heads that turned as she held hands on the way out to the parking area. My car had been delivered to the airport and was waiting for us in a reserved spot near the loading zone. "You look so fucking HOT in your uniform," Greta told me as I slid into the driver's seat. "Not as HOT as you look in that dress," I chuckled my reply. Greta reached over and laid her hand on my thigh. "I can't wait to have you rip it off me...and shove that big beautiful cock into my cunt," she said in a sultry voice. She used her other hand to pull up the front of her dress so I could see her bare gash. "My pussy has been waiting for you for three years," she whispered.

I pulled in to the first Hotel that I saw as we left the airport. We decided that dinner could wait. We both had a much deeper hunger to satisfy. Greta kissed me very tenderly when we got into the room. "There's something I've been wanting to tell you," she whispered as she stepped back to wiggle out of her dress. "I love you, Trevor." She said it softly. "Oh God.... look at how lovely you are," I gasped as I gazed up and down her gorgeous body.

The upturn of her 34B breasts looked so exquisitely sensuous. Especially with those huge puffy nipples. There was a small white triangle between her legs and across the top half of her ass from her bikini bottoms. Greta has always sunbathed topless but prefers to wear her bottoms just in case the neighbors peek at her. Which of course they do at any opportunity. Greta is a perfect 34-20-32 and her shiny white blond hair is still as silky as the day I met her years ago.

"I love you too," my voice trembled as I said it. Greta placed the palm of her right hand in the middle of my chest and began to gently push me backwards towards the bed. "I meant that I am IN LOVE with you," she informed me. "And, I am not your mom...remember," she chuckled it as she pushed me back till I was seated at the foot of the bed. My heart was racing from her words now. She was in love with me!

"I love you too, Greta...I always have...as long as I can remember," I blurted out. "I know, baby," she said it as she began to untie my combat boots. I began to unbutton my shirt as she pulled off my boots and socks. She started to unbutton my pants as I pulled my t-shirt off over my head.

"Oh Trevor...look at you," she gasped as her eyes wandered up and down my muscular body.

For the last three years I have lifted weights and done calisthenics on a daily basis. I have jogged at least five miles per day. My 6 foot 2 body is chiseled and deeply tanned from the endless hot sunny days in Afghanistan. There isn't an ounce of fat on my 195 pound frame. "Oooh Trevor," she moaned softly as her free hand reached up to pet my chest. She stepped back and pulled my pants off along with my boxers.

"Look at thaaaaaat," she giggled playfully as her hand reached out to touch my throbbing 9 inch prick. I was now completely naked with Greta for the very first time. All the other times where on camera. But this time, we were in the same room and she had her hand – petting my cock. "I have fantasized about this moment my entire life," I moaned softly. I felt her hand gently pushing on my chest again.

"Scoot back, sweetheart," she instructed. Again my heart palpitated from her calling me her sweetheart. I scooted back till my head was on the pillows. "I've thought about this for a very long time too," she whispered as she crawled onto the bed between my legs. "Oooh Greta," I gasped as I felt her mouth engulfing my cock. I can't even describe how sensual she looked as her body slowly moved back and forth while she sucked on my prick. Her long silky hair brushed back and forth against my legs.

I was deeply aroused as she raised her head and a long strand of precum stretched from her lower lip all the way to my pee hole. "Ooooh geezus, you are so fucking sexy," I groaned. Greta slowly scooted up so my dick was perched just under her smooth bare gash. "I need to have you inside me," she whispered. "Oooh my God yes," I moaned as she lowered herself till I was all the way inside of her drenched slit.

My body was quivering with arousal as my deepest fantasy was now becoming a reality. The sensation of her hot drenched pussy gripping my dick was electrifying for me. More dazzling than even my imagination could ever have created. It thrilled me that her body was trembling just as much mine. "God, I've wanted this," she purred softly.

"You are my first, Greta." The deep love that swept across her face as I said it made it well worth the wait. "You are the only one I have ever wanted to do this with," I told her as I pulled her forward to kiss her. Greta kissed me so passionately that I thought she would suck my toes out of my mouth. "Oh Trevor....I will never forget this...ever," she panted when she finally let me gasp for some air.

I bent my head down so I could suck on her wonderful puffy nipples while she began to hump back and forth on my raging hardon. The pillowy softness of her nipples was very erotic to me.

I could feel her hot juices flooding down onto my thighs as she humped on my dick. "Oh Trevor, Ooooh Trevor," she moaned over and over. It fascinated me to play with her nipples and suck on them. I had dreamed of this for so many years.

Besides being in incredible physical condition due to my daily work out, I also have built up an unbelievable stamina. Greta rode my prick for nearly twenty minutes and I felt her quiver into several climaxes. Each time she did, there was a small gush of fluid that ran down onto my thighs. "Ooooh fuck yes," she grunted when I flipped her over onto her back. I pushed her feet all the way back to either side of her head and pressed forward until I was buried even deeper inside of her.

"Fuck me, Trevor...Fuck me," she moaned in a deep husky voice. Smack, smack, smack, smack. My hardened belly slapped forcefully against hers as I pounded myself into her over and over and over. "Take me, take me, take me," she grunted with each brutal thrust. I held myself up so I could see myself impaling my beautiful Swedish step mother. So

I could see every inch of her beauty beneath me. "You...are...so...fucking...gorgeous," I grunted out.

Although I had fantasized for many years that I would spray my cum on her sexy tits, I decided that since this was our first time and my very first time, I would leave my dick inside of her. "Here it is...here it is," I screamed as I began to ejaculate. My cock spasmed four times flooding her pussy with my semen. I felt her body jerk and quiver as she felt the heat of my seed bathing the inner reaches of her vagina. "Ooooh Trevor...Yesssss, yesssss," she moaned.

I was ecstatic that I had just given my manhood to Greta. I was glad that I had waited for her. That she could be my first. "I'm in love with you too," I whispered hoarsely as I fell forward to catch my breath. "I will remember this forever too." It was so unbelievable to me that I was finally able to have my fantasy come true. It felt incredible that she had wanted that too.

Chapter 3

I had to run out to the Mercedes to get our luggage so we could put on some clean clothes to go out for dinner. I threw on my fatigue pants and tank top t-shirt. The sort that used to be called a "wife – beater" shirt. There was a sexy young redhead just pulling her luggage from her car next to mine as I opened my trunk. "Look at you...welcome home GI," she flirted.

"I'm sure would love to give you a special homecoming," she pulled down the front of her tube top to expose her 36C tits to me. At another place and time I might have considered her offer. But I had just made love to the only woman I have ever wanted and she was waiting for me even now. "Sorry...I'm taken, Hun," I called over to her. "But I am flattered by your offer," I added. "I'm in room 19 if you change your mind," she told me as she pulled her top back up. "Maybe your gal would agree to share you with me," she smiled wickedly as she said it.

I noticed the curtains open slightly to room 19 as Greta and I got into the car. Greta and I had just put on jeans to go out for dinner. Hers were those new low rider skinny jeans that cling to the legs and allow you to see the top of her ass cheeks. Her top was one of those halter tops that ties around the neck and in back just below her breast level. The fabric in front just hangs down loosely in a triangle to cover the breast and the tip of the triangle barely hangs down above her bellybutton. She looked sexy as hell.

I have to confess that my dick got hard as I imagined my Greta muff diving on that cute little Irish looking redhead as we drove to the diner. I told Greta about the encounter while we were eating dinner. I decided that she and I should never have any secrets of any sorts. Even the most harmless secrets can sometimes come back to bite you in the ass.

"Oh Trevor...that might be fun," Greta replied to my shocked surprise. "It is so special that you waited all these years for me...I'd like to do something special for you," she added. I was blown away. Not only did I have the sexiest woman on earth, but she was willing to do a threesome with me. I tried not to wolf down my meal, but I did eat very quickly that night.

"I'll be right back," she told me when we got back to the hotel. She was knocking on the door of room 19 as I stepped into our room two doors down. I felt like a teenage boy waiting for his first date as I waited for Greta to return. I was worried that the young woman might be intimidated by another woman coming to answer her offer. Especially when that woman is so incredibly sexy like my Greta. "She'll be here in fifteen minutes," Greta announced when she came into our room. She sounded excited as she said it.

When Greta came out of the bathroom from getting ready for our guest, she was wearing a peach colored transparent baby doll nightie. "I bought this just for you," she told me as she slowly spun around so I could see every inch of her beauty. "You like my peach colored robe so much," she giggled. I was stretched out on the huge king size bed when we heard the knock on the door.

"I'll get it," Greta announced. I sat back against the headboard in the middle of the bed and used my bath towel to cover my manhood.

"So glad you wanted to join us, Amanda," Greta greeted her as she let Amanda into the room. As soon as the door was closed, they fell into an embrace and began to French kiss passionately while their hands greedily petted and fondled each other. My dick was hard as steel and poking out the front of the towel within seconds. "Oh My God, that's HOT," I gasped softly.

I heard whispering and giggling as they stepped back from each other. It thrilled me when Amanda slowly unbuttoned the front of her light tan summer dress then let it fall off to the floor. She was completely naked as Greta bent forward to suck gently on one of her dark pink nipples.

As she moved to suck on the other one, Amanda reached down to untie the top of Greta's nightie so it fell down to her waist. "Let's go play with Trevor," Greta giggled as she wiggled out of her nightie. They kissed one more time then both crawled onto the bed with me.

"You can have him first," Greta whispered as she leaned over to kiss Amanda on the cheek. I felt Amanda's hand gently wrap around the girth of my twitching prick. "Look at this," she gasped. She bent forward and flicked the tip on my dick with her wet tongue. "This will be fabulous," she she added. "Ooooh Geezus, yes," I groaned as she sucked my dick in her mouth.

Greta leaned over my face so I could suck on her tits while Amanda sucked on my prick. I had never imagined anything so extraordinary. The sensation of two gorgeous women both pleasing me at the same time was spectacular. "Ooooh, fuck yes," I groaned when Amanda scooted up and impaled herself on my cock.

Greta gently swung her leg over my head and scooted down till her pussy was inches from my mouth. The musky scent of her arousal was intoxicating to me, just like her panties had been when she mailed them to me. "Oooooh my God yes, Trevor," she moaned when I began to hungrily eat her cunt. It electrified me to see Amanda's hands pinching and pulling on Greta's nipples while she sucked on the side of her neck and rocked back and forth on my dick. The expression on Greta's was pure erotic lust.

"Eat me Trevor...Eat my cunt," she wailed. As her cunt muscles had spasm after spasm, I could feel her fluids running down my thighs. "Make me cum...Make me cum," Greta bellowed. I felt a huge gush of fluid as Amanda climaxed again. "Oooh my God," Amanda moaned in a lusty voice.

"Oh yes baby...I'm cumming...I'm cuuuummmmming," Greta screamed. I felt her body go rigid and then she was jerking uncontrollably as I sucked on her clit unrelentingly. "Oh Yes Baby, Oh yes...Oh my God yes," Greta screamed breathlessly. Amanda was still having spasms as my dick began to ejaculate deep into her quivering hole. "Oooooh Yes, Trevor...Yessss, yesssss," Amanda moaned in a deeply guttural tone. I felt a gush of hot fluid spray into my face at the same moment that Amanda sprayed all over my belly and thighs. My dick shot one more load up into Amanda's vibrating cunt.

Amanda spent the night with us. After we had rested, she climbed on my face so she was facing Greta and they kissed and fondled each other's breasts while Greta humped my prick. It was so fucking erotic to watch them enjoying each other as they both fucked me. We slept very soundly with me spooned between the two of them. Greta in front with my hands cupped around her breasts. Amanda behind me with her tits mashed against my back and my ass pressed against her belly. It felt so marvelous.

I heard moaning when I woke up the next morning. When I opened my eyes, I could see Amanda seated in the big stuffed chair in the corner of the room. Her legs were propped up on the padded arms of the chair spreading her legs wide open for Greta who was hungrily lapping at Amanda's sloppy wet sex hole. Amanda had both hands behind her head gripping the back of the chair as her head thrashed back and forth. "So good, Greta...soooooo good," Amanda moaned softly.

My cock swelled to full erection as I gazed at Greta on her knees. The milky white skin on her ass from her tan line looked so erotic as she wiggled her ass back and forth. "Oh my God yes," Amanda cried out as Greta shoved two fingers up into her gash. I crawled out of bed and scooted up behind Greta. "Yesss, my love," Greta purred when I slid my hand between her legs from behind and rubbed my palm up and down her dripping slit.

I bent down and pried her ass cheeks apart with my hands. "Oooooh Trevor," it was a deep husky moan as I darted my tongue in and out of her sex. "Oooooh my God, yes," her entire body shook when I drug my tongue up to her ass pucker and poked the tip inside. For the next several minutes I slobbered on her ass pucker and shoved my tongue further and further inside of her. "FUCK ME TREVOR...PLEASE FUCK ME," she bellowed.

I scooted forward and shoved my dick into her drenched pussy till I was buried to the root. "Oh my God, yes," she groaned. Greta now had four fingers buried inside of Amanda's cunt and was banging her savagely with her entire hand. Smack, smack, smack, smack. The sound of my thighs pounding against Greta's ass filled the room.

I held Greta's hips with both hands and drove myself as deep into her with each thrust as I could reach. Amanda was convulsing on the stuffed chair as Greta brutally fucked her with her hand. "OH FUCK, YESSSSSSSS," Amanda screamed as she wet herself. It thrilled me to see Amanda's urine spraying all over Greta's face and tits. I shoved all the way in one last thrust and vibrated as my dick erupted again and again and again. I felt a gush of fluid as Greta had her climax too.

"Good morning, then," I panted as I pulled my dick out of Greta. They both giggled at that. Greta and Amanda took a shower together before Amanda got dressed to leave. I thought it best to let them enjoy the time alone before we would have to say goodbye. They took a long shower. I heard giggles and moans. I heard deep throaty gasps of lust. Amanda gave me a deep passionate kiss before she left. "Thank you for reconsidering that offer," she told me softly.

"This was even better than I could have imagined," she added.

Greta and I took our time traveling the distance to our home in Seattle. We spent a night in Nashville and the next in Denver. Then we took two days to travel down to see the Arches National Monument in southern Utah. It was a bit out of the way, but both of us really wanted to experience that together. And this was a week of new experiences for me. First ever sex with my stepmother, first threesome, first blow job while driving and first sex in public. We found a small cave in the National

Forest and fucked our brains out while there were other visitors walking around just outside.

Our last stop for the night before arriving home was Boise, Idaho. We selected a hotel just off of Interstate 15 next to the airport. We ended up on the top floor facing another hotel across the street that was a couple of levels taller. It was just after dark when we stepped out onto the patio balcony. I had stripped down to just my boxer shorts and Greta had removed everything except her see through white nylon panties.

"You know I'm crazy about you," I whispered into her ear as I fondled her perky tits from behind. As she leaned her head back so I could kiss on the side of her neck, I saw a man directly across from us on his balcony two levels above us. He was staring down on us. His eyes were riveted to my hand squeezing Greta's tits. "Yesss, Baby," she purred as I rolled her nipples between my fingers.

I could see the man calling to someone inside his room and his arm as making a come here sort of gesture while I continued to twist and pull on Greta's swollen nubs. He was quickly joined by three other men on his patio. They proceeded to pass a pair of binoculars back and forth as they all gawked at us. "We have company," I whispered as I slid one hand down into her panties. "Oh yes,baby," she cooed when I slipped a finger up into her dripping sex. I felt her quiver.

"Pull my panties down and fuck me right here in front of them," she moaned softly. "That's my girl," I whispered in her ear as both hands grasped the waist of her panties and slowly wiggled them down to her knees. "Ooooh Yes, Trevor," her pussy was sloppy wet as I shoved my dick up into slit. I very slowly pulled all the way back and then slowly pressed all the way in. I fucked her like this for several minutes so the men would have a good view of my dick slipping in and out of her pussy. Although I did not look at them directly. I could see that all four of them were jerking off now as they continued to watch.

As I grabbed her hips so I could fuck her more forcefully, Greta reached down between her legs and began to finger herself as I pounded into her. "Fuck me, fuck me, fuck me," she grunted with each brutal thrust. I could feel the load building up in my balls as I heard each of the men grunted and groaned as they spewed their cum all over the balcony they were standing on.

"YES BABY...GIVE IT TO ME...GIVE IT TO ME," Greta yelled it loud enough for them to hear as I started to spray my semen deep into her womb. "Oh my God, Yes," she gasped as the heat of my fluid sent her over the edge too. "That was so nasty," she giggled when she turned around into my arms to kiss me. I mashed her ass cheeks as she kissed me so the men would have one more view before we went inside and closed our drapes. "That was incredible," I chuckled once we were alone in the room.

We went to sleep early that night. We were now running out of steam after the many miles we have traveled. It would be a ten hour drive from Boise to Seattle. We needed some rest so we could get an early start. We had a quickie in the shower before calling room service for our breakfast. We were on the way home by 7 am.

The four hour drive to Pendleton OR was scenic but boring. About half way across the long mountainous drive, Greta reached over and gave me a hand job. It was thrilling to feel her hand jerking me off as we sped along at 70MPH and even more arousing when a trucker pulled next to us to watch what she was doing. I reached down and pulled her tube top down so he could see her tits. I was ecstatic when she sat up and wiped my cum all over her tits after I shot off in her hand. The look on the truckers face was priceless.

We were just coming over Manastash Ridge, when Greta unfastened her jeans and wiggled them down to her knees. "I'm so fucking horny," she groaned as she began to masturbate. It would be at least two more hours before we were home and neither of us knew if dad would be home or not. There was a forest road off ramp coming up on our right. I pulled off and drove the Mercedes up a dirt road where there was some privacy from the expressway.

We practically jumped out of the car as soon as I had it shut off. I had her get on her knees on the passenger seat and drove my cock into her from behind. "Oh God I need you," she gasped as I impaled her. I fucked her very slowly at first. All the way in and all the way out. It mesmerized me to see my dick shoving in and out of the woman I have fantasized about for so many years.

"I will never get tired of this," I whispered as I reached around to mash on her tits. "I won't either," she moaned her reply. When I felt her quivering near her climax, I pressed my thumb into her ass pucker. "Oooh God yes," she screamed as I unloaded three wads of cum into her hole.

Chapter 4

It turned out that it was a good thing that we stopped and screwed in the Canyon. Dad was not due to be home for several more days, but there he was. We knew that we would have to deal with his presence around the house from time to time, but we were not ready for this surprise. We had both wanted to screw some more...in our own house for the first time.

"Frank...you look...well," Greta sounded surprised as he walked out to the Mercedes. "Nice ride," he called into me through the passenger side as she stepped out. He seemed to ignore the fact that her top was completely open exposing her tits. In my mind, I thought "Damn nice ride and the car's nice too." But my reply was "Thank you Dad."

By the time dad and I got into the house, Greta had fixed her blouse. Although she did not button it up, she had tied the bottom in a loose knot under her breasts. Don't I even get a hug?" she asked dad. He almost seemed annoyed as he stepped forward to give her quick little pat on the back sort of hug. I was amazed that even despite being a part for three weeks, that was the best he could do. No kiss, no warm embrace and no intimate squeeze of the rump.

I was just lugging in my two duffle bags when dads cell phone began to ring. It was an old song that he had selected as a ringtone for this caller. "I had the time of my life," blared out and dad quickly muted it as he made his way to the stairs. "I have to...take this call," he grumbled as he started up towards his den. "Yes...Yes...just a minute," his voice sounded secretive. Greta was in the kitchen and did not hear it.

"I missed you, Greta," I whispered in her ear as I reached around to cup her tits from behind.

"Daddy's upstairs talking to his special friend," I let one hand slip down into the front of her jeans.

She trembled as I unbuttoned her jeans so I could rub on her bare pussy. "I wanted to show you how happy I am to be home," I felt her shudder as I inserted two fingers into her pussy. "Oh Yes, Trevor," she gasped softly.

It was so erotic to be fondling her and fingering her gash in this kitchen. The same kitchen where I have gawked at her and fantasized about her for so many years. The added danger of my dad being right upstairs made it even more intense. "I want you fuck you," Greta moaned softly. I just drove my fingers in faster. "Later my love...this is for you," I whispered.

My dick was hard as granite and I desperately wanted to yank her jeans down and screw her till we both couldn't walk. But that was too risky and this way I could just step away if we heard him coming. With her back to the door, she would have time to fix her pants like nothing happened.

I ground my bulge against her ass while I humped her gash with my fingers. It felt wonderful to feel her body pressed against me as she jerked and spasmed through her climax. I lifted my fingers to my mouth and sucked them dry. "You taste so good," I whispered.

Greta had just finished buttoning up her jeans when dad entered the kitchen. I was glad that I was seated at the table where he could not see the raging bulge in my jeans. I cringed when he stepped behind Greta and fondled her ass while he kissed the side of her neck. "Not now, Frank," she pushed his hand off her rump.

"Really?" It was more of a statement rather than a question. "You didn't call me in three weeks and now you expect me to just jump in the sack?" I saw dad look back at me over his shoulder as he whispered something in her ear. "Maybe I WOULD fuck him...if he ever asked." Greta was getting angry now. "I bet he would know how to please a woman in bed." She turned to face him.

"Something you haven't done in years."

I pretended that I was reading the sports page as he turned and left the kitchen in a huff. Greta and I were eating our late dinner when he came back down stairs and announced that he was going out for drinks. "Sure good to have you home, son." It was the first time he had spoken to me since he complimented my car. That's the way it has always been with him and me. "It's wonderful to be home," I glanced over at Greta as I said it. He never saw that..he was already halfway out the door.

Greta jumped out of her chair the moment we heard his car leave the driveway. We both knew he would be gone at least two hours. Either he would really go to the country club and have drinks with his cronies. Or he would go down to the Porn Arcade in the seedy part of town to get a blow job from one of the hookers that hang around the Arcade. Either way, he would be gone a couple of hours.

"Fuck me...I can't wait another minute," Greta gasped as she jumped into my arms. I lifted her into my arms and kissed her neck. "In my room...I want to fuck you in my bed," I told her softly.

I had an idea as I carried her up the stairs. "Tonight was our Skype night," I reminded her. "How would you feel about putting on one more show for them?" "Oooh sweetheart, that would be so yummy," she replied eagerly.

I quickly sent a text message to one of my buddies back at the encampment. I told him that there would be a special Skype show in 15 minutes and to collect as many of the fellas that he could round up. I told him this would be a freebie as a gift from Greta and me. We were both very giddy as we prepared for our live sex show.

I placed my laptop on the dresser right next to the bed where the guys would be able to see all of the action on the bed. I arranged the lighting so it was directed down onto the bed so there would be a very clear picture for the hookup. I logged onto the site and then placed it in a pause mode with the remote and waited for the arranged time. When I pushed the resume button on the remote, I could see that the tent was filled with guys. There must have been at least two dozen young soldiers packed into my old home away from home.

"It's so good to be home…," that was the cue for Greta to walk into the room in her peach colored transparent nightie. "I have a special welcome home for you," she answered as she came into view of the camera. There was a chorus of groans from the laptop as the men gawked at her nude body through the transparent fabric.

There was another chorus of groans when she sat down on the edge of the bed and placed her hand on my throbbing prick. "Look at my baby stand to attention," she giggled as she yanked my thong down to expose my erect prick. I could now hear slapping noises as many of the men began to jerk off. I could tell by the way Greta's hand was trembling that she was very aroused.

I heard a few grunts as a few of the men creamed themselves already. "Suck it..suck it for me," I moaned as her head bobbed up and down. I could hear many groans in the background as the astonishment of our sex show aroused the men further and further. I pulled her top down and was squeezing on her bare breasts as she sat back up. "But you promised to fuck me," she said it in a naughty tone.

There was a very loud groan as many of the fellas had watched us play on the skype before and had heard me tell her I wanted to fuck her. "You promised," she reminded them as she moved up to straddle my lap. I reached forward and yanked open her snap crotch and she slowly lowered herself so the men could clearly see every inch of my cock slip inside of her. I heard some more grunts as some of men shot off.

"Fuck me, Trevor…fill my cunt," she bellowed. I lost track of the men on the screen for a while after that as I just enjoyed watching Greta ride my prick. I pinched and pulled gently on her puffy nipples while her hands were pulling at her scalp. She was putting on quite a show for the boys. As soon as I felt her quiver into her first little climax, I flipped her over onto her back and drove my dick all the way into her gash.

"Oh God yes...Fuck me, fuck me." It was that deep throaty moan that thrills me beyond words. Smack, smack, smack, smack. I pounded into her brutally as I felt the load collecting in my balls.

"On my tits baby...cum on my tits," she wailed as she felt me beginning to vibrate. At the last moment, I yanked out of her and got on my knees. I could hear many men grunting as my cum shot out of my prick and sprayed all over Greta's gorgeous tits. Some even sprayed all the way up onto her throat and chin.

After I rolled off of her, Greta sat up and faced the camera so the fellas had a great view of the cum all over her tits and throat. "I waited three years for this," she told the viewers. She used her fingers to smear my cum all over her chest. She used two fingers to pinch her dripping nipples and then shoved the two fingers into her mouth like she was sucking a cock. "You taste so good, baby," she took another lick on her finger. "Next time, I want you to shoot in my mouth," she said it very seductively.

As soon as I hit the off button, I tossed the remote on the floor and pulled her back down on the bed. "Now it's your turn, sweetie," I told her as I hovered over her. I bent forward and kissed her passionately for a moment then moved down to greedily suck all the cum off her tits and throat.

"Yes baby, yesssss," she purred as her hands pressed my head more firmly against her tits. I felt her quiver with excitement as I inserted a finger into her drenched sex hole.

"I have always wanted this," I mumbled as I scooted down to her honey pot. "Me tooooo, Oh my God...meeeee toooooo," she moaned as I began to twirl my tongue around inside her dripping cunt. I took my time and very slowly brought her to the brink of orgasm and then moved back to bite gently on her thigh until the urgency subsided. "Oooh you tease," she gasped.

I inserted two fingers into her gash and gently fingered her while I teased her clit with just the tip of my tongue. "Oooh geezus, that's good...sooooo good," she moaned. Her hands were now pressing my face into her sex hole. Her legs were vibrating from her arousal. "Don't stop..pleeeeze don't stop," she groaned. Her pussy was gushing her arousal all over my face. I gently bit down on her swollen clit and began to suck on it.

"OH MY...FUCK YES...OH MY GOD YES," she screamed and her body began to jerk and flop all over the bed. I crawled forward and shoved my dick all the way inside of her and held it there while she convulsed beneath me. The sensation of her spasms gripping my dick was fantastic.

Without moving an inch, her cunt milked the cum right out of my prick. "Oh, fuck yes," I moaned as I flooded her womb with my semen.

Greta was in the shower cleaning up when dad returned. If he had come anywhere near me he would easily have smelled the sex all over me. "See you in the morning," he waved to me as he passed the living room and went directly upstairs. I had mixed emotions as I watched him going up to their room. His hurry to get upstairs meant that he did not go to get a blow job. He would be wanting to fuck Greta. In the back of my mind, I smiled. He would have my cum all over his dick after he had his way. But Greta would have to suffer through the five minutes of his selfishness.

The next two days were excruciating for us. Dad was home most of the time and even when he went out there was no way of telling how long he might be gone. Although we managed to steal some passionate kisses and enjoy some moments of heavy petting, it was too risky to attempt screwing each other. It was a little cat and mouse game we played. I would touch her ass while she was cooking dinner. She would touch my cock while he was taking out the trash. We kept each other on pins and needles much of the time.

Added to our misery was the fact that dad wanted to fuck her as soon as they went to bed each night. I tried to block out the sound of the bed springs screeching and the low guttural grunt that signaled that he was flooding her with his seed. I tried to block out how desperately I wanted to go yank him off her and tell him that he doesn't deserve her. But in my heart, I knew that Greta was suffering much more than I was. I knew it must be hell to lay there and let a man take you selfishly when there was no intimacy left to speak of.

It was Saturday morning when dad announced he would be leaving for Baltimore in the evening. He said he needed to get an early start for his business meeting scheduled for Monday morning.

As I glanced at Greta, I could tell that she wanted to jump out of her chair and scream for joy just like I did. "How long will you be gone this time?" I was blown away by how casually she was able to say it. I had to bite my tongue to stifle the excitement when he told her, "Five weeks, maybe more."

I heard Greta humming softly that day as she went about her chores. Dad was in and out alot with his preparations for his trip. Although Greta laid out all his clean clothes and arranged his suits in a neat row, he has always insisted on packing his own luggage and making all of the arrangements himself.

Greta had shown me his laundry when he first got home. There were several of his underwear that had obvious cum stains in them and a couple of his dress shirts had lipstick smudges on them. It is very obvious that there is something sexual going on with him and someone else. Greta told me that it has been this way for nearly five years. Any last feelings of guilt that I felt evaporated after that.

I felt Greta running her bare foot up to my crotch as we all ate an early dinner together. Dad seemed almost giddy as he chattered on about his important business meeting. Greta had my dick twitching under her toes and I could see a slight grin on her face as she tried to act like she was paying attention.

"You make sure you take care of your mom," I almost creamed in my jeans as he slapped me on the shoulder unexpectedly. "Keep her happy for me, son...take care of her needs while I'm gone," he added with another little pat on the shoulder. I could feel the precum oozing into my silk thong as her toes rubbed the head of my prick. "I will tend to her every need, dad," I replied softly. I had a shiver as I felt some of my seminal fluid running down my right inner thigh. There was a gleam in Greta's eyes as she lifted her foot away. "We will get along just fine, dear." She smiled as she wiped the corner of her mouth with her napkin.

I helped dad carry his luggage out to the car. He would have porters to carry them at the airport and again when he reaches Baltimore. "I am proud of what you accomplished in the Army," he told me as he got into his chauffeured limo. "But I am happy that nonsense is finally over."

He glanced up before the man came to close his door. "Now go make something out of yourself," he growled as the man swung the door closed.

I was between Greta's legs before his limo reached the end of the block. Added to the desperate need that we had both suppressed for the last two days, I was filled with anger at my selfish and overbearing father. "I'm fucking your wife asshole," I grunted as I pounded into Greta. "I'm fucking your gorgeous son," Greta groaned her reply. We humped violently on the couch until we were both spent. "Fuck him!" I panted as we finally rested. "No baby...I'd much rather fuck you," Greta whispered. She held me very tenderly as we laid there and rested for quite some time afterward.

Chapter 5

The next two weeks were like a honeymoon for Greta and me. I reveled in the fact that we rarely wore clothes. It was so stimulating to watch her every move and to be able to just walk over and caress her lovely nakedness anytime I wanted to. It was heavenly to feel her hands exploring my body unexpectedly as I was busy with some chore or concern. The very torrid sex that we have shared began to take on a beautiful intimacy as the days progressed. "I really am very deeply in love with you," I confided softly as we were curled up watching TV on that second Saturday night.

"Prove it," she whispered softly as she turned into my arms. Her gorgeous perky breasts were mashed into chest as she gently kissed the side of my neck. I could feel the heat of her breath just under my ear. "Make a baby with me, Trevor." Her warm slender fingers were fondling my soft prick. "Put a baby in my belly and make me yours forever." She sucked on my earlobe as she said it. My cock was now fully rigid in her soft warm palm.

As I rolled Greta over onto her back, she had the most wonderful glow in her face that I had ever seen. It was the look of a deep and all-consuming love. "Yesssss," she moaned softly as I slowly slid my cock up inside of her. I felt her fingers gently grasping my shoulders as I drove myself into her till I was completely buried in her sex hole.

Although we have played together hundreds of times on skype and have screwed our brains for most of the last month, this felt entirely different this time. It felt brand new. It felt like the very first time again. Except that this time there was a deep love that was connecting us together in an emotional bond that mirrored the sensation of her vagina grasping my prick.

As I slowly pulled out and then pressed forward, it felt like I could feel every molecule of her being wrapped around me like a warm radiating tenderness. "Yesss, baby, yesss," she moaned in my my ear as her fingernails dug into my flesh. I kissed her neck very tenderly while I seesawed my engorged prick in and out very slowly.

I was enraptured with the intense intimacy of this moment. I wanted this exquisite familiarity to last till the end of time. I could feel her heart pounding in unison with mine. I could hear the soft tremble in her breath. I could feel the heat burning in her sex.

I'm not really sure how long we mated. We were both lathered in sweat and panting deeply for air as I felt my seed begin to flood into her womb. It felt like a torrential tidal wave that swept through me and gushed into her like an endless river. My entire body vibrated as I emptied myself into her. It felt like I filled her with every particle of my being. I rolled onto my side and we laid there just wrapped in each other's arms for quite a while.

"Are you sure you want this?" I asked her softly when we crawled into bed that night. For the first time, I felt a little inadequate. I questioned my ability to be a husband and father. "I don't even have a job yet," I added timidly. Greta reached over and held my face in her hands. "You will do fine, sweetheart." She gently kissed my forehead as she said it. "You will be a wonderful father," she added after a second kiss. She reminded me that even if she took a fraction of my dad's wealth in a divorce, that we could live comfortably for quite some time.

We really had no idea how we were going to make it work that night as we fell asleep entwined together. We only knew that we were in love and the rest would have to work itself out somehow. Neither one of us could have ever guessed that dad had already done most of the work for us. It was only up to us to find the evidence that would make him agreeable. I felt more happy that night than I could ever remember since my mother had died.

We received a card in the mail that next morning from the fellas in my unit. Inside the card was a check for two thousand dollars. My friend Pete explained that the fellas had enjoyed our Skype show so much that they had taken up a collection for us. "The fellas want you to take your mom somewhere special for Mother's Day," Pete advised.

Greta and I were thrilled with the gift. With Mother's Day just a few days away and dad gone for at least another two weeks, we could easily slip away for a week alone somewhere. We decided on Las Vegas without a second thought. We made the arrangement to fly out that afternoon.

Greta looked breathtaking for our trip to Las Vegas. She wore a very tight faded blue jeans with high heels which made her long legs look magnificent. Her top was a white transparent leotard and she wore a matching short blue jean vest to cover enough of her breasts to avoid creating a scandal. Her long Swedish blonde hair was pulled into a long ponytail that reached all the way down to her rear end. Many heads turned as we made our way through the Seatac airport.

"You really are the most beautiful woman on earth," I whispered to her as we took our seats in first class. "You're just saying that because you love me," she whispered back. "But you can keep saying it," she added with a giggle. I leaned over and kissed her on the cheek. As I looked down, I got a terrific view of her gorgeous tits through the transparent fabric. "Did I mention that you have great tits?" I teased her. There was a gleam in her eyes as she kissed me back.

There seemed to be a bit of confusion when we arrived at the fancy casino to check in. The man at the front desk informed me that I had already checked into the hotel two days earlier. When I told him that wasn't possible since I had just made the reservations this morning, he checked his ledger again and discovered I had a different first name than the gentleman that checked in two days ago with his wife Peggy.

We had our luggage delivered up to our room and then went to have an early dinner at the 5-star hotel restaurant. We had just ordered our meal and I felt the pressure of Greta's bare foot slowly rubbing up my thigh towards my crotch. "I need a date with Mr. Happy," Greta giggled softly.

My dick was quickly swelling in my jeans. From two tables in front of us, I heard a voice that I could not possibly ever mistaken. It was the other man with my last name in this hotel. It was my dad. Since his back was to us, he had no idea that his wife and son were just two tables away. His assistant Peggy was so busy petting on him and whispering in his ear, that she wouldn't see us if we were two feet away.

"I think our answer has presented itself," I whispered to Greta. I felt her wiggle her toes against my twitching bulge. Peggy was nibbling on dad's ear as Greta rubbed her foot up and down the length of my rigidness. "I bet I'll have a lot more fun than she will tonight," Greta giggled. "Oooh God," I moaned as I watched Peggy suck on my dad's neck. I watched as my father put his hand under the table and slip it between Peggy's legs. Her legs parted and I saw her shudder slightly.

As our meal was being delivered, I overheard dad tell his waiter to charge his meal to his room. Greta and I both smiled at each other when he announced his room number. It was the room next to ours with a door that connects the two rooms. I noticed a devilish look on Greta's face as she pulled out her cell phone. She winked at me as she dialed the numbers.

I nearly spit out my wine when I heard the alert song that dad had for Greta's phone number. It was the "wicked witch" jingle from The Wizard of Oz. "Honey...I was going to call you." I could hear him even without Greta's phone. It was hilarious to watch the annoyance on Peggy's face and the way her body language changed so drastically.

"I miss you so much baby," Greta announced. "I was thinking that maybe I could come join you in Baltimore," she taunted him coyly. She winked at me as she said it. There was a pause while dad got over the shock and tried to figure out how to respond. Peggy was shifting her weight back and forth nervously and holding on to his left arm like it was a life preserver. "NOT EVEN POSSIBLE," dad nearly shouted it. "I WOULD NOT HAVE TIME FOR YOU IF YOU CAME TO VISIT."

"Oh...so it would be just the same as when you are home," Greta goaded him. "I guess you're right...it would be a waste of time." Greta hung up before he could say anything more. "What did she say...What did she say?" Peggy was ranting as they left the restaurant. I could see a grin on Greta's face as she watched them leave. "They will be perfect for each other," she whispered.

By the time we ate and made it up to our room, it had been almost 45 minutes since Peggy and dad had left the restaurant. I poked my head out of the elevator when it opened on the 8th floor to be sure the coast was clear. Then Greta and I quickly ran to our room. We could hear moaning coming from dad's room the minute we had our door closed. "Soooo good...Soooo good," It was dad's voice in a deep guttural moan.

SMACK-SMACK...

"You love having your ass fucked, huh," Peggy cackled wickedly. SMACK-SMACK...

"Oh my God yes," SMACK. "Oh my God yes." We could hear the quiver in dad's voice.

"OH FRANK...YOU WET YOURSELF," Peggy laughed crudely. Greta and I just looked at each other in astonished disbelief. "Oh God yes...Fuck me...Fuck me," dad wailed.

SMACK-SMACK-SMACK...

"Oooooh Peggy...Yesssss," he moaned in that deep primal voice again. "Yes, Frank...give it to me...cum on my big tits." We could hear slapping sounds as she jerked him off to climax. "Oh my God Peggy...Oh my God yes," he screamed.

Greta and I just stood there next to the door between the two rooms completely spellbound. There was a long silence and we heard a squeak like someone is getting off the bed. "You can untie me now," we heard dad groan softly. "NOT UNTIL YOU TELL THAT LITTLE BITCH THAT YOU ARE DIVORCING HER," Peggy yelled at him. There was another short silence and it sounded like he was struggling on the bed.

"Okay...bring me my cell phone." His voice sounded resigned. Like it was inevitable. Like he was relieved to finally make the decision. I saw Greta fumble to shut off her ring tone so the phone would only vibrate. I turned on the bathroom fan to block out the sound of the vibration as her phone buzzed in her hand. "What is it Frank?" Greta answered the call.

Greta had a sad look on her face as Frank told her they were through. Her final understanding of why her husband has been so cold and distant all these years. The reason he stayed away for many weeks at a time. The reason her sex life has been so unfulfilling for so very long. "Call me back in ten minutes and I will give you my answer," she said it softly and then hung up. We could hear Penny nagging at him for an answer. "What did she say...What did she say?" She bellowed.

Greta sat her phone on the dresser then kicked off her heels. "Are you okay, hun?' I asked softly. Greta lifted her head and smiled at me as she began to unbutton her jeans. "I want you to take me out on that balcony and fuck me like you own me," she whispered as she wiggled her jeans down and then stepped out of them.

As she began to pull her leotard down and wiggle out of it, my dick began to swell. "Oh my God, I love you," I gasped softly. "Yes baby, I'm okay...this means I can be all yours." She answered me finally. "Now, get those clothes off and fuck me." She said it playfully. I quickly stripped down till I was naked and we went out on the patio. It was still very warm even though it was after 10 pm.

I sat down on the chaise lounge and Greta swung her legs over me so she could lower herself onto my rigid prick. "Ooooh Greta," I moaned softly. The silky hot wetness of her sex engulfed me completely as she slid down till I was buried inside of her. I kissed her passionately as she got into a nice rocking rhythm on my prick. The warm air had us both dripping with sweat with a couple of short minutes.

I was greedily sucking back and forth on Greta's nipples when her cell phone rang. Greta never stopped humping as she answered dad's call. "Go out on your balcony, Frank...and you'll find your answer." She pressed the off button then dropped her cell phone onto the concrete patio floor. "Fuck Me Trevor, Give me a baby." Smack, smack, smack, smack. As her ass pounded down against my thighs, I faintly heard dad's patio door opening to his balcony.

"FUCK ME...FUCK ME....FUCK ME," I yelled loud enough for him to hear. I saw him freeze as he saw me with Greta impaled on my prick. "WHAT...THE...FUUUUUUCK?" The sound in his voice was astonished confusion. Greta never stopped riding my dick as she pulled his ring off her finger and tossed it to him. He was so stunned that he never moved. The ring bounced off his chest and fell to his feet.

"There's your answer asshole," she groaned as she continued to grind herself on my throbbing pole. "Tell your hag she's welcome to you...I got a much better offer." It was at that moment that Peggy stepped out onto the balcony. Her 38DD tits squeezed tightly in a black corset and her black thong panties pulled so far to one side we could see her gash.

Peggy froze as she glanced over and saw Greta riding my dick. I grabbed Greta's ass and lifted her up higher and higher so they could both see my cock sliding in and out of Greta's sex hole. "Fuck me...Fuck me," I gasped loudly. "Oooh Geeeeezus," Peggy gasped. I could see that Peggy was gawking at every inch of my muscular chiseled body as I lifted Greta up off the lounge chair and forcefully bounced her up and down on my prick "Oh my," she gasped softly. She had one hand partially covering her mouth as she stared at us.

Greta seemed thrilled that I picked her up. She wrapped her legs around my waist and her arms around my neck. "Yes Trevor...put a baby in my belly," she moaned as I shoved her up and down on my oozing cock. Dad suddenly fell backwards as his knees buckled and he landed on his lounge chair. "Here it is Greta...here's my seed," I yelled as I began to ejaculate deep into her womb.

"What would your mother think?" Dad asked in a hoarse crackly voice. "I think she would be pleased that I found a wonderful woman that loves me," I told him without hesitation. "I think she would be happy that I am free of you now," I added. I pulled Greta off my dick and sat her back on her feet. We stood there naked in front of him. "You made your choice dad and I made mine," I told him softly. "I wish you both all the happiness in the world." I told him. "I already have that with Greta."

THE END

Here is a sample from another story you may enjoy:

JACK RYDER

The Second
Honeymoon

EROTIC ROMANCE

It was just at the end of what the baseball players call the "Dog Days of Summer" which would be towards the end of August. In fact, it was precisely the third Friday in August and I had just been informed that my publisher had just cut me a very hefty bonus check due to the very successful sales of my newest release. And this, just days after my wife Darcy had brought home a very nice commission check on the property she had sold the week before.

With this sudden windfall of extra cash, Darcy and I sat down and had a long conversation about possible things we could use the money for. In our early forties now with both kids off at college, we have enjoyed the "empty nest" time together. After a very long lull in our sexual relationship, we had just started to get back into the romance and passion that we had once had with each other.

We had recently made several trips to the local lingerie stores and to a local Adult Arcade to purchase items to spice up our love life. We had also day dreamed a bit about doing some traveling together. It would be wonderful without the kids under foot. We would be free to come and go as we pleased and frolic sexually...like a second honeymoon.

It was during this conversation that we came up with the idea of purchasing a Motorhome. The sort you drive around like a bus. With the amount of cash we had just pulled in, we could easily afford one and have plenty left for travel expenses. After dinner that night, we began a search on line. We were flabbergasted by the amount of different types and sizes that were available. We were also astounded by the many price ranges for these MotorCoach Vehicles.

After visiting a half dozen dealerships and reviewing common prices online, Darcy and I chose a used vehicle over the many newer ones available. The Monarch Motor Coach that we chose was only 5 years old, it only had 35k miles on it and it was only one third the price of what a newer vehicle would have cost. Although we could have afforded to buy a new vehicle, the money we saved would allow us to replace both of our aging cars and allow us plenty of money for a one month vacation. And now...we had the mode of transportation!

It was a fifty dollar taxi ride to Salt Lake City to take ownership of the Monarch. We had made arrangements to pick it up there since it had been transported from Houston and the man that delivered it would need to catch a flight home. We were like a couple of giddy teenagers as we stepped into our new bus. It was even more pristine than the photos had illustrated. The previous owners had obviously taken very good care of the MotorCoach!

"Pull in over there!" Darcy suddenly exclaimed when we were almost home. The area that she pointed to was the parking lot of the mall just off the freeway. As soon as I had us parked way in the back of the lot, she grabbed my hand and pulled me back towards the bedroom. "I have something I want to show you!" she sort of giggled it as she pushed me down onto the bed. I watched in amazement as she pulled off her sweater and then her loose fitting sweatpants. She giggled again playfully when she saw the look on my face as I gazed up and down her body.

Under her sweatpants and sweater, Darcy had worn a very sexy pink babydoll nighty. It was the kind that has a snap in the crotch and the top ties around the neck. It was completely see through. Her 34B-25-34 body looked sexy as hell as I glanced at her. I could feel that my dick was swelling quickly as she reached down to begin unfastening my jeans. "We need to break in this new bed!" she giggled. "I just can't possibly wait another moment!" she whispered.

"Ooooh, Darcy...Yesssss!" The sensation of her mouth engulfing my prick was electrifying. I hadn't felt this aroused and this animated since the very first time we had been together back in college. I gently fondled both of her breasts through the soft fabric of her nightie as she slowly bounced her head up and down. The wetness of her drool running down my shaft was fantastic.

"You ready to fuck me, stud muffin?" She chuckled it as she moved up and unsnapped the crotch of her nightie. It thrilled me! She hasn't called me that since before our daughter was born 20 years ago. "Ooooh, Daaaaaaarcy," I moaned as her pussy enveloped my prick till I was buried all the way to my balls. Her arousal was oozing and running down my thighs. The fact that we were fucking in the mall parking lot in broad daylight stirred me even more.

"Oooh God, Jason. Oh fuck. You feel so hard!" Darcy purred as she began to lift up and then shove back down onto my rigidness. It felt glorious to feel her trembling with such arousal and the steady flow of her juices pouring onto my thighs. It has been many years since we have had this sort of sexual passion between us. "Fuck me, baby. Fuck me!" I whispered. I reached up and began to squeeze on both her tits. She reached up and pulled her top down to bare her breasts for me. "Yes. Yesssss!" Her entire body was quivering as I gently pinched and pulled on both of her nipples.

Splat, splat, splat, splat...the sound of her ass slamming down onto my drenched thighs was so erotic to me. It felt so marvelous to have my wife so aroused...so completely enthralled with the passion that was now transpiring. When I felt her body beginning to jerk into orgasm, I raised up and buried my face in her tits as she bucked and screamed out her pleasure.

The sensation of her vaginal muscles stroking my cock as she flexed and relaxed was marvelous! "Oooooh yesssssss!" My cock erupted deep inside her womb, flooding her with my hot sticky semen. The kiss that Darcy gave me after we finished was the most passionate kiss we had shared in many years. Although she put her sweatpants back on for the drive home, she chose to not put her sweater back on. I got a very good view of her breasts all the way home.

The next two weeks were excruciating for us while we waited to begin our trip. We did not want to be on the road during the Labor Day Holiday. The traffic would be just too much to deal with and all of the RV parks and locations we wanted to visit would be too over crowded.

So we had decided to wait until the Tuesday after the Holiday for the start of our honeymoon. This allowed us time to conclude some business deals that we were involved in separately and it gave me time to stock the Motorcoach with all the supplies and equipment we would need to be mostly self-supporting over the next month.

The Monarch Motorcoach was better than anything we had imagined. The 36-foot bus is powered by a Ford V10 gas engine that has more power than I ever dreamed. The cabin has two slide outs to create more room for the living room area and bedroom. The sleeper sofa opens up into a queen sized bed every bit as large as the bed in the back bedroom. The cabin power is supplied by an Onan gas generator. The kitchen is fully self-contained with 3-burner stove, an oven and a microwave.

There are many extra perks that include the two-door fridge with ice maker, the satellite dish on the roof for the TVs in the living room and bedroom. There are DVD players and music systems for both rooms and there is a separate outside shower hook up to go along with the indoor shower in the bathroom. Both sides of the Motorcoach have retractable awnings for added shade while outdoors. There is a backup camera that allows one to see behind the bus from the comfort of the huge cushy driver's seat.

Almost every day of that two weeks, we found excuses to go out and "check on something" in the bus. Mostly just to see it, be inside of it, enjoy that it was real! We spent many of those times kissing and petting and frolicking like a couple of teenagers in a special secret place. Just this one new thing in our lives had stirred up a newness and passion for us that was exhilarating and adventurous for both of us!

We left just before noon on that Tuesday. The trip down to Moab and the Arches National onument area would only take about 4 hours. We would have plenty of time to select a nice private spot in any of the RV areas that would be available. We could even unhook the Jeep we were towing to run into town for a restaurant meal if we wanted. We found a perfect RV site just as we entered the town. It was right along the bank of the river and was completely empty when we paid for the two nights' lodging fee.

After we freshened up a bit, we unhooked the jeep and drove into town for dinner. It was just a pizza joint, but it felt good to be out among other people for a little while. I made it a point to only have one beer with dinner. I wanted to be at peak performance for our first night in the bus. Our first "second honeymoon!" We were both a bit disappointed when we found another Motorcoach parked right next to ours when we returned to the RV park. "All those open spaces and they had to pick the one right next to us!" I muttered as I parked the jeep. The Winnebago seemed like it couldn't possibly be any closer to ours as we walked towards the front entry door.

"Hi ya! I'm Jim and this here is my Jasmine!" They were suddenly approaching us from the front of the Winnebago. They looked like a couple in their late 40s. Jasmine was a tall woman, probably about 5 foot 8 and had a rack that was at least a 38DD. She has obviously taken very good care of her voluptuous body and her tits were obviously silicone. "Actually, my name is Jamie. The other name was my stage name!" She seemed to smile a little as she said it. There seemed to be a sparkle in her eyes too.

"I met this little woman 20 years ago at the Boom Boom club humping poles and making the men crazy," Jim laughed crudely. "Knew right away I would want her forever!" he chuckled. "It took some doing to get her attention though!" She gave him a gentle pat on the rump. "All you had to do is pay off my parole officer," she giggled in a naughty tone. Darcy and I looked at each other with that sort of glance that says, "Ok TMI," but we both just smiled and shook our heads as if we understood them completely.

Before we could make our way into our Motorcoach, they insisted that we join them for a quick nightcap in their Winnebago. It was only a little after 9pm so we figured it would be a quickie and we could soon be in our bed. As we chatted and had several drinks, rather than the one they had first mentioned, it seemed to me that they were sort of flirting with us. Neither Darcy nor I had ever had an experience like this.

About an hour later, Jaime excused herself for a moment to use the bathroom. When she came back, she had removed the sweat pants that she had been wearing and changed her top as well. She was wearing a very tiny bikini bottom and a cutoff t-shirt that barely covered her massive jugs. "Just had to get more comfortable," she giggled softly as she sat back down on the couch across from us.

As the conversation continued, I noticed that each time she reached forward to get her drink from the coffee table. I could see all of her big round tits poke out from under the shirt. They really were lovely tits and I had a difficult time not staring at them. Her bikini bottom was so tiny that I could see her pussy lips pressed around the side of the little slit of fabric that was wedged into her gash. It was becoming very uncomfortable as I felt my pecker beginning to swell. But I could not keep my mind from wondering what it would be like to have her wrapped around my body and feel those jugs in my face and have my cock buried in that lovely crack.

Just before we finally made our excuses to leave, Jim mentioned something about him and Jamie being players. "We are always on the lookout for new adventures," he told us. I felt the softness of Jamie's hand on my back as we went to the door. "I'd love to play with you, Jason!" She whispered it in my ear as her hand moved to squeezed gently on my ass. I noticed that Jim was whispering something in Darcy's ear at about the same time. It appeared that his right hand was up around her breasts but I could not tell from behind. I heard Darcy giggle softly as his hand moved back to his side.

If you enjoyed this sample then look for The Second Honeymoon.

Also by this Author

The Handyman Seduction

The Beer Bust Scandal

Scandalous Emotion

Intimate Relation

The Seduction of Kimi

Erotic Goes Hi-Tech

One at a Time

The Wizard Casey's Coven

The Inn Keeper's Wizard: When Love and Magic

Collide

Trailer Trash Payback

Queer Intentions

Zoe's Fun House

Public Display

Test Drive

Breaking the Bonds

Trailer Trash Payback

The Hero's Welcome

The Twenty-Eight Day Cure

The Cougar Club

The Wife Swap

In Love with a Cougar

Stella for Christmas

The Long Ride Home

A Shot at Love

The Second Honeymoon

About the Author

Jack Ryder LOVES everything there is about sex!

When he is not involved with his "swinger" friends, enjoying a steamy threesome, or being part of a raunchy "gang bang", you can find him on first class planes, trains, and cruise ships. Traveling seems to be the BEST way to finding new and interesting sexmates for him. Sexmates. Plural. He lives with the saying "The More, The Merrier!"

He owns a successful business in New York. He writes as a hobby and also as sort of documentation of his mind-blowing sexcapades over the years. He is presently roaming around the streets of Manhattan but can be anywhere in the world too, since he travels often. So, beware! You just might be his next mate.

"The most fun thing I enjoy when writing my stories is trying to figure out which is fantasy and which was memory. ENJOY! (Preferably with a friend. *wink*)" -Jack Ryder-

From the Author

If you have any comments, suggestions, or would just like to get a little personal, please feel free to email me at:
jack_ryder@awesomeauthors.org

If you enjoyed any of my books then please share the love and click like on my books in Amazon.

If you write me a review and send me an email I will send you a free book, or many.
(Just know that these emails are filtered by my publisher.)

Good news is always welcome.

One Last Thing, For Kindle Readers...

When you turn the page, Kindle will give you the opportunity to rate this book and share your thoughts on Facebook and Twitter. If you enjoyed my writings, would you please take a few seconds to let your friends know about it? Because... when they enjoy they will be grateful to you and so will I.

Thank You!

Jack Ryder
jack_ryder@awesomeauthors.org